First published in Great Britain in 1985 by
The Bodley Head Children's Books

This edition published in Great Britain and in the USA in 2008 by
Frances Lincoln Children's Books, 4 Torriano Mews,
Torriano Avenue, London NW5 2RZ
www.franceslincoln.com

British Library Cataloguing in Publication Data
available on request

ISBN 978-1-84507-723-5

Printed in Singapore

9 8 7 6 5 4 3 2 1

COMING TO TEA

Sarah Garland

F

FRANCES LINCOLN
CHILDREN'S BOOKS

Roll the biscuits,
mix the cake,

and bake the tarts for tea.

Are you ready next door?

Here they come.

Over the fence,

and into
the sandpit.

Tea's ready!

Mmm… delicious…

but down comes the rain.

Quick, come in!

A long chat, then it's time
to go home.